For my big family, I am so fortunate.
And for Keith, my favorite person to
ring in the New Year with!
—KM

For all my families in China.
—XY

 little bee books

New York, NY
Text copyright © 2022 by Katrina Moore • Illustrations copyright © 2022 by Xindi Yan
All rights reserved, including the right of reproduction in whole or in part in any form.
Library of Congress Cataloging-in-Publication Data is available upon request
For more information about special discounts on bulk purchases,
please contact Little Bee Books at sales@littlebeebooks.com.
Manufactured in China   RRD 0722
First Edition   10 9 8 7 6 5 4 3 2 1
ISBN 978-1-4998-1282-4 (hc)
ISBN 978-1-4998-1422-4 (ebook)

littlebeebooks.com

Grumpy New Year

by
Katrina moore

illustrated by
XinDi YAn

little bee books

10 DAYS until the new year . . .

Daisy hugged her parents goodbye.
"This will be the best Lunar New Year ever!"
Daisy was visiting her grandpa in China.
They would have so much fun together!

"Remember, Auntie will
drop you off with Yeh-Yeh.
You should sleep on the long flight,"
said Mama.

Daisy *should* have slept—
but she didn't.
She was too excited to see Yeh-Yeh!

9 DAYS until the new year . . .

8 DAYS until the new year . . .

"We're here, we're here!"

"Jó sun," said Yeh-Yeh.

After unpacking, Yeh-Yeh showed Daisy
his favorite spot to fly a kite.
"Ahh . . . " said Yeh-Yeh.

"Gah!" grumbled Daisy.

That night, Yeh-Yeh said, "Fun găo."
Daisy *should* have slept—

but she didn't.
There were too many new things to explore!

7 DAYS until the new year . . .

Yeh-Yeh planned a
fun-filled day for Daisy.
First, they painted with ink.

Then, they sang karaoke.
But that didn't last too long.

Finally, they rode a boat.

Nothing was as fun as Daisy hoped.
Why am I being such a grump?!
Will I make Yeh-Yeh grumpy, too?

6 DAYS until the new year . . .

Yeh-Yeh took Daisy to his favorite restaurant.
Yeh-Yeh *slurped.* Yeh-Yeh *burped.*
Daisy wanted to smile—
but she didn't.

"AHH!" yelled Daisy. She pointed to the fish head.

Then . . . *CHOP!*

"Harrumph," Yeh-Yeh grumbled.

At night, Yeh-Yeh said, "Fun găo."
Daisy *should* have slept—

but again, she didn't.
There were too many sights to see!

Daisy couldn't get rid of the grumps,
not even while making yummy rice cakes with Yeh-Yeh.

"Nián gāo," said Yeh-Yeh. His hands danced.
Stir. Whirl. Pour.

Daisy rolled onto the floor.
RRR! GROWL! ROAR!
"Hmmm," Yeh-Yeh grumbled.
He patted Daisy's head. "*Fun găo.*"
Daisy needed to sleep—

and finally, she did.

4 DAYS until the new year . . .

3 DAYS until the new year . . .

Daisy woke up in time to make . . .

"Zong zi!" Yeh-Yeh announced.

"What about the dumplings?!"
Daisy asked.
Yeh-Yeh pointed.

"*Boo*," Daisy grumbled.
"I missed it."

2 DAYS until the new year . . .

Daisy did not want to miss a thing today!
"I'm ready!" Daisy cheered.
Yeh-Yeh handed her a broom.
"Oh," Daisy grumbled.
It was time to clean before the new year.
Daisy dusted. She swept. She *sighed*.

This day wasn't turning out
like Daisy hoped. Until . . .

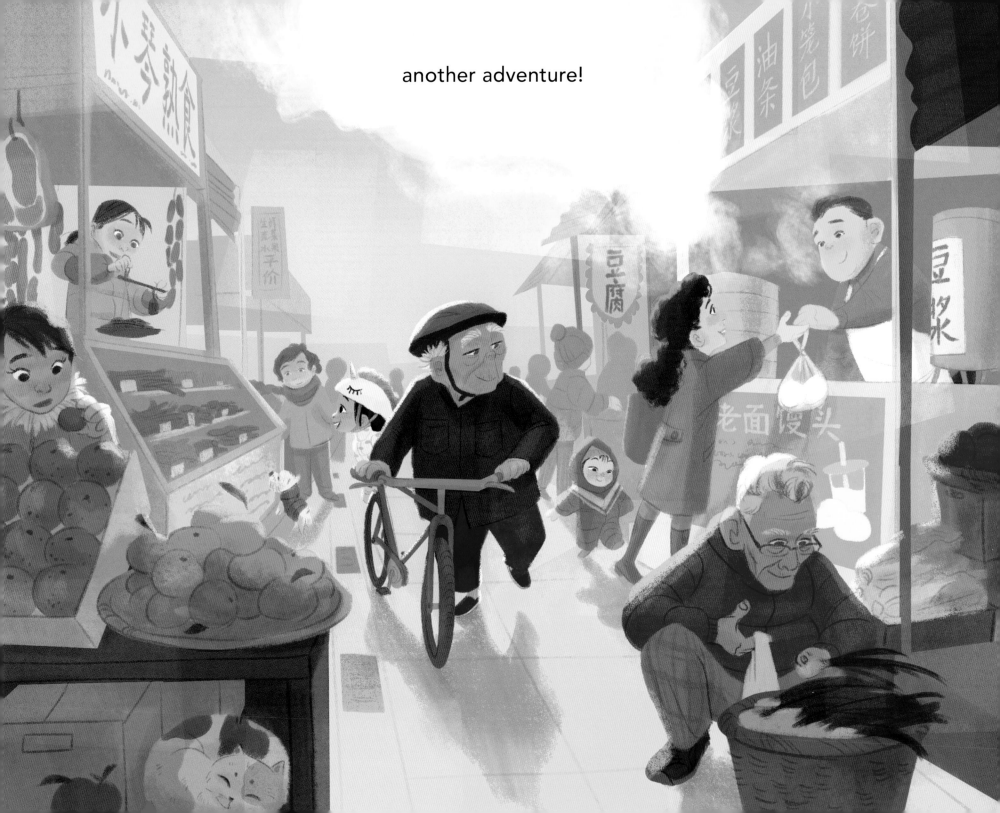

another adventure!

Daisy loved the market.
"Oranges!" she cheered. She tried a slice.

Sweet. Juicy. Tangy.
"Mmm," said Daisy.

She handed one to Yeh-Yeh.

"Gah!" grumbled Yeh-Yeh. He scrunched up his face.
Daisy tried not to—
but she couldn't help but . . . *smile.*
Soon, Daisy and Yeh-Yeh were laughing so hard,
his belly jiggled up and down.

1 DAY until the new year . . .

Daisy ate and ate,

and danced and danced.

By the time she went to bed, she finally felt jolly again . . .

On New Year's Day . . .

Daisy stretched her arms.
She smelled something sweet, like tangy oranges,
as well as something steamy, like zong zi.
Something sizzled—dumplings, fresh from the wok.
The breezy air buzzed with jingles and jangles and jovial voices.

"Oh, no!" she cried. "Did I miss the new year?"

Daisy peeked into Yeh-Yeh's room. No Yeh-Yeh . . .
What was this? Lucky money, *but no Yeh-Yeh*.

*Yeh-Yeh wants to celebrate
the new year without me*, thought Daisy.
Maybe I've been too grumpy.

But, wait—what was *this*? A map?!

Daisy hoped she would find Yeh-Yeh. . . .

And she did.

"Gōng hei fat choi!" said Yeh-Yeh.

10 . . . 9 . . . 8 . . . 7 . . . 6 . . . 5 . . .

4 . . . 3 . . . 2 . . . 1 . . . "Happy New Year!" cheered Daisy.

Celebrating Lunar New Year!

Author's Note:

Growing up, the only thing that made me grumpy about Lunar New Year was that I had to clean my room. Actually, having to clean up still makes me grumpy! But everything else about celebrating the New Year was full of joy, and most importantly, family. I grew up in a big-big-big Cantonese and English-speaking Chinese-American family, and we were always eating, or thinking about eating food. My Yeh-Yeh would begin the New Year's food preparations the days leading up to the first night of Lunar New Year. The whole house was abuzz with sizzling, splashing, stirring, stuffing . . . and sweet and salty smells. When it was finally "midnight" of the first night of the New Year, my family would gather around our kitchen table for a feast of long noodles, fish, sweet rice cakes, "snowball" soup, and various types of dumplings, including my favorite, fried Jiao Zi!

Yeh-Yeh's Fried Jiao Zi

1 handful of shredded cabbage
1 ½ tsp. minced ginger root
¼ handful of minced green onions
　(optional)
1 ½ tsp. sesame oil

¼ lbs. ground meat (my favorite is pork and shrimp)
A pinch of white pepper
30 dumpling wrappers
　(sometimes called dumpling skin)
½ tsp. soy sauce

(*This recipe should be made with adult supervision. Children should stay away from a hot stove!*)

1. In a bowl, mix all the ingredients (except the dumpling wrappers). Stir slowly until all are combined. Mix well.
2. Lay the wrappers out on a clean, slightly floured tabletop.
3. Place a small portion of the filling into the middle of each wrapper. Fold the dough over the filling into a half moon shape and pinch the edge to seal. Crimp or fold the edges over to make fun edges. Get creative!
4. Repeat steps 4-5 until you run out of filling. The recipe should make approximately 30 dumplings.
5. To cook the dumplings, boil water in large pot.
6. Once the water boils, add the dumplings (a small batch at a time). When the dumplings float to the top, they are ready. Remove the dumplings from the water and set aside. Add the next batch and repeat until all the dumplings are boiled.
7. Over medium heat, fry the dumplings in a pan or wok with vegetable oil until they are crisped and browned to your liking.
8. Serve with your favorite dumpling sauce and enjoy!

Lunar New Year was my favorite holiday tradition growing up in China. It lasts for fifteen days, and a lot of shops and markets were closed for the entire time. So we needed to buy and cook enough food for the whole family to last (and I was allowed extra snacks and candies). I loved following my mom around on the back of her scooter to the produce markets and shops, listening to the buzzing crowd and seeing the festive red holiday decorations everywhere. Whenever we ran into a friend, we'd greet each other with a big happy "Xin Nian Kuai Le!" (Happy New Year!) or "Gong Xi Fa Cai!" (May the New Year bring you prosperity!) Chinese people love to put meanings of good luck and prosperity into everything, especially when it comes to the Lunar New Year. You would see that in a lot of holiday food; for example, the circular shape of a sticky rice ball symbolizes a harmonious family reunion (Tuan Yuan). The Eight Treasure Rice was our favorite as kids. It's sweet with candied fruits and a red bean paste filling. As you can tell from the name, it symbolizes our wish for a rich fruitful New Year.

Eight Treasure Rice

For the rice
1 cup sticky rice (glutinous rice)
1 handful of various dried fruits and nuts such as dried dates, raisins, cranberries, apricots, pumpkin seeds, etc.
(As it's named eight treasures, it would be fun to add eight different ingredients, but it's not required. Eight is a lucky number in Chinese culture. I would also recommend crushing or chopping bigger ingredients, like peanuts or walnuts, for a better texture and taste.)
2 tbsp. butter/cooking oil
¼ cup sugar
3–4 tbsp. red bean paste (you can find this in Asian supermarkets or make your own with red beans, sugar, and butter.)

For the glaze
2-3 tbsp. sugar
¼ cup water
½ tsp. corn starch

(*This recipe should be made with adult supervision. Children should stay away from a hot stove!*)

1. Cook the sticky rice. You can soak the rice for 30 minutes and cook in a rice cooker. If you don't have a rice cooker, soak the rice overnight. Drain and spread onto a steamer basket. Cover and steam for 30-45 min until the rice is cooked through.
2. While the rice is cooking, brush a big bowl with oil and start arranging the dried fruits and nuts. Traditionally we arrange them in a concentric circle. But feel free to get creative and come up with your own designs!
3. Once the rice is done cooking and while it's still hot, mix in the butter/cooking oil and sugar.
4. Scoop half of the rice into the bowl and carefully place on top of the fruits. Press down with your spatula.
5. Scoop in the red bean paste and spread in the middle.
6. Spread and pack in the rest of the rice.
7. You can eat it cold by putting the bowl in the fridge until cool, or eat it hot by steaming it for about 30 min in the bowl.
8. Make the glaze by combining sugar and water till the mixture is boiling. Dilute the corn starch with a tablespoon of cold water, pour into the syrup, and cook until boiling again.
9. Flip the bowl of eight treasure rice over onto a plate. You should see your beautiful design on top now. Pour on the sugar glaze and enjoy!